Shakespeare's Plays

THE EARLY PERIOD, 1588-1594

Comedies	The Comedy of Errors
	Love's Labour's Lost
	The Two Gentlemen of Verona
	The Taming of the Shrew
History Plays	Henry the Sixth, Part 1
	Henry the Sixth, Part 2
	Henry the Sixth, Part 3
	Richard the Third
Tragedies	Titus Andronicus
	Romeo and Juliet

THE PERIOD OF 1595-1601

Dramatic and Comic Plays	A Midsummer Night's Dream
	The Merchant of Venice
	Much Ado About Nothing
	The Merry Wives of Windsor
	As You Like It
	Twelfth Night
History Plays	Richard the Second
	Henry the Fourth, Part 1
	Henry the Fourth, Part 2
	Henry the Fifth
	King John
Tragedies	Julius Caesar
	Hamlet

THE PERIOD OF 1602-1608

Comedies	All's Well That Ends Well
	Measure for Measure
Tragedies	Troilus and Cressida
	Othello
	King Lear
	Timon of Athens
	Macbeth
	Antony and Cleopatra
	Coriolanus

THE PERIOD OF 1609-1613

Romantic Dramas	Pericles
	Cymbeline
	The Winter's Tale
	The Tempest
	The Two Noble Kinsmen
History Play	Henry the Eighth

Hear, Hear, Mr. Shakespeare

Story, illustrations, and selections from Shakespeare's plays
by Bruce Koscielniak

Tell me where is fancy bred,
Or in the heart, or in the head?
How begot, how nourished?
Reply, reply.

(song) - The Merchant of Venice 3:2

Houghton Mifflin Company   Boston 1998

For M.R.
—B.K.

The author wishes to acknowledge gratefully that
the Shakespeare quotations in this book are taken principally from the following editions:

Craig, Hardin, ed. THE COMPLETE WORKS OF SHAKESPEARE.
Scott, Foresman and Co., 1961.
Evans, G. Blakemore, textual ed. THE RIVERSIDE SHAKESPEARE.
Houghton Mifflin Co., 1974.

The text of this book is set in Pabst.
The Shakespeare quotations are hand-lettered by the author.
The illustrations are ink and watercolor on paper.

LIBRARY OF CONGRESS CATALOGING-IN-PUBLICATION DATA
Koscielniak, Bruce.
Hear, hear, Mr. Shakespeare : story, illustrations, and selections from Shakespeare's plays / by Bruce Koscielniak.
p. cm.
Summary: Players on their way to London to perform for the queen stop in Stratford-on-Avon
to visit William Shakespeare. Includes related quotations from Shakespeare's plays.
ISBN 0-395-87495-5
1. Shakespeare, William, 1564–1616—Juvenile fiction.
[1. Shakespeare, William, 1564–1616—Fiction. 2. Actors and actresses—Fiction.] I. Title.
PZ7.K9555Fo 1998
[Fic]—dc21 97-14775 CIP AC

Printed in Singapore
TWP 10 9 8 7 6 5 4 3 2 1

Hear, Hear, Mr. Shakespeare

To the reader:

Though much about the life of the playwright and poet William Shakespeare (1564-1616) is not known, it is fairly certain that during most of his life he was connected to the small market town of Stratford-upon-Avon, in central England. In this green, rural community, Shakespeare may well have spent relaxing hours, away from his writing, by tending his garden.

The reader is invited to make a fanciful visit with Shakespeare at his Stratford house and garden and to savor the rich texture of his words.

"Hear, hear, Mr. Shakespeare.
Sing along. All sing along.
We bring good cheer-a," called the players as they approached.

"Hear, hear, Mr. Shakespeare.
O woe! O woe! Our one and only play—a very fine comedy
called A Very Fine Comedy of Blunders—is washed away with rain.
Can you hastily write for us some jolly new play?" asked the players.

...friends we'll hear a play....
– Hamlet 2:2

Acting troupes had to buy their
plays from an author, if they had
no author in their company.

"Hear, hear, Mr. Shakespeare. Our good queen visits fair Stratford to ask if you may have some new play to bring to London town. Your last play brought much delight!" called the coach driver.

Too nice, and yet too true!
— Macbeth 4:3

What reply, ha?
—Measure for Measure 3:2

A great while ago the world begun,
With hey, ho, the wind and the rain,
But that's all one, our play is done,
And we'll strive to please you every day.

♪ ♪♪♪ ♩ (song) –Twelfth Night 5:1

If we do meet again, we'll smile indeed;
If not, 'tis true this parting was well made.
–Julius Caesar 5:1

And towards London they do bend their course....
–Richard the Third 4:5

Shakespeare's Dates

1564   William Shakespeare is baptized on April 26 at Holy Trinity Church, Stratford, England. Popular tradition gives Shakespeare's birthday as April 23.

1582   Shakespeare marries Anne Hathaway at Stratford. (Children: Susanna is born 1583; Hamnet and Judith, twins, are born 1585.)

1593   Shakespeare is at work in London as a poet, playwright, and actor. A little volume containing two of his poems is published in London.

1597   Now a busy and successful dramatist in London, Shakespeare purchases a large house, called New Place, near Guild Chapel in Stratford.

1599   Shakespeare, along with other members of the acting company to which he belongs, called the Chamberlain's Men, becomes part owner in a new London playhouse, the Globe Theatre.

The Globe was a custom-built public theatre, probably round or octagonal in shape, with no roof over the center. On the ground level was a raised stage and an open area for a standing audience, and there was seating available in two upper galleries.

1602   Shakespeare's company plays before Queen Elizabeth I several times during the Christmas season. Elizabeth (for whom the Elizabethan Age is named) did much to promote Shakespeare's work.

1613   Shakespeare retires from his work in the theatre and returns to a quiet life in Stratford.

1616   Shakespeare dies on April 23 and is buried two days later in Holy Trinity Church, Stratford.

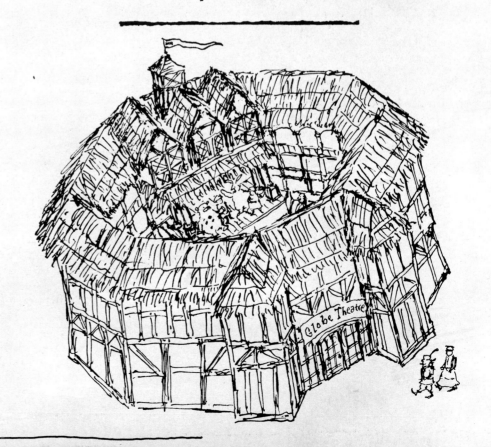

Globe Theatre